The Tiara Club

Also in the Tiara Club

Princess Charlotte *and the* Birthday Ball

Princess Katie *and the* Silver Pony

Princess Daisy *and the* Dazzling Dragon

Princess Sophia *and the* Sparkling Surprise

Princess Emily *and the* Substitute Fairy

VIVIAN FRENCH

The Tiara Club

Princess Alice
AND THE
Magical Mirror

ILLUSTRATED BY SARAH GIBB

KATHERINE TEGEN BOOKS
An Imprint of HarperCollins*Publishers*

The Tiara Club: Princess Alice and the Magical Mirror
Text copyright © 2007 by Vivian French
Illustrations copyright © 2007 by Sarah Gibb
address HarperCollins Children's Books, a division of
HarperCollins Publishers, 1350 Avenue of the Americas, New
York, NY 10019.
www.harpercollinschildrens.com

Library of Congress Cataloging-in-Publication Data
French, Vivian.
Princess Alice and the magical mirror / by Vivian French ;
illustrated by Sarah Gibb.
    p.   cm.— (The Tiara Club ; 4)
Summary: Princess Alice determines to take responsibility
when she causes another princess to drop and shatter a vase dur-
ing the school's preparation for the term garden party.
ISBN-10: 0-06-112440-0 (trade bdg.)
ISBN-13: 978-0-06-112440-2 (trade bdg.)
ISBN-10: 0-06-112439-7 (pbk.)
ISBN-13: 978-0-06-112439-6 (pbk.)
    [1.   Princesses—Fiction. 2.   Responsibility—Fiction.
3. Magic—Fiction. 4. Schools—Fiction.] I. Gibb, Sarah, ill.
II. Title.
PZ7.F88917 Pral 2007   2006019223
[Fic]—dc22   CIP
                                                      AC

Typography by Amy Ryan

❖

First U.S. edition, 2007

For Princess Alice of Orchard,
with lots of love, x
—V.F.

For Alan, Lucy, and Steph
—S.G.

The Royal Palace Academy
for the Preparation of Perfect Princesses
(Known to our students as "The Princess Academy")

OUR SCHOOL MOTTO:
A Perfect Princess always thinks of others before herself,
and is kind, caring, and truthful.

We offer the complete curriculum
for all princesses, including:

How to Talk to a Dragon

Creative Cooking for Perfect Palace Parties

Wishes, and How to Use Them Wisely

Designing and Creating the Perfect Ball Gown

Avoiding Magical Mistakes

Descending a Staircase as if Floating on Air

Our principal, Queen Gloriana, is present at all times, and students are in the excellent care of the school Fairy Godmother.

VISITING TUTORS AND EXPERTS INCLUDE:

KING PERCIVAL *(Dragons)*

LADY VICTORIA *(Banquets)*

QUEEN MOTHER MATILDA *(Etiquette, Posture, and Poise)*

THE GRAND HIGH DUCHESS DELIA *(Fashion)*

We award tiara points to encourage
our princesses toward the next level.
Each princess who earns enough points
in her first year is welcomed to the
Tiara Club and presented with a silver tiara.

Tiara Club princesses are invited to return
next year to Silver Towers, our very special
residence for Perfect Princesses, where they
may continue their education at a higher level.

PLEASE NOTE:
Princesses are expected to arrive
at the Academy with a *minimum* of:

TWENTY BALL GOWNS
*(with all necessary hoops,
petticoats, etc.)*

TWELVE DAY-DRESSES

SEVEN GOWNS
*suitable for garden parties
and other special daytime
occasions*

TWELVE TIARAS

DANCING SHOES
five pairs

VELVET SLIPPERS
three pairs

RIDING BOOTS
two pairs

*Cloaks, muffs, stoles, gloves,
and other essential
accessories, as required*

Hi! I've been longing to meet you—you're the best! Not like horrible Princess Perfecta and Princess Floreen. Sometimes they're so spiteful! My big sister says it's because Perfecta didn't get nearly enough tiara points to join the Tiara Club last year, so now she's back in the first year with us. Poor us!

I'm Princess Alice, by the way. I'm learning to be a Perfect Princess at the Princess Academy, just like you, but you know what school is like—hard work! If it weren't for Charlotte, Katie, Emily, Daisy, and Sophia, I think I'd collapse. And I don't know about you, but I just can't be good all the time. . . .

Chapter One

*H*ave you ever been to a Garden
Party? We have one every term here
at the Princess Academy, and they
are so much fun—at least, that's
what my big sister says. She says
everyone dresses up in their very
best dresses and tiaras, and a huge

orchestra arrives to play dance music, and the fountains splash sparkling lemonade. There are flowers everywhere, and all our relatives are invited to come and see us. And if it looks like rain, guess what happens? Fairy G.—that's the school Fairy Godmother— floats a sunny blue sky over the whole garden! Isn't that amazing?

There's another fantastic thing about the Garden Party. It's the one and only time when Fairy G. brings out the Princess Academy Magical Mirror . . . and it really is magical. My big sister made me promise I wouldn't tell anyone what happens because it's supposed to be a really big surprise, but I know it's okay to tell you. This is what happens. . . .

On Garden Party day, every princess in the Princess Academy puts on one of her special dresses, does her hair, and puts on her tiara. Then each princess is invited into Fairy G.'s private study to curtsey to her reflection.

And guess what?

The Magical Mirror looks right back and decides how much of a Perfect Princess you are—and it gives you tiara points. And it can give you up to three hundred! But my big sister says nobody has *ever* gotten that many.

So you can see why I was count-ing every single minute until Garden Party day, but of course there was a bad side to it as well.

Suddenly we had dozens of extra classes in *Curtseying to the Floor*, and *Walking Gracefully in Long Skirts*, and *Dancing*. We had to learn *hundreds* of new dances! It

seemed as if we never had even half a second to relax. But we did our best, and at last there was only one day to go. Our dresses were already hanging up in our dormitory. My

dress was very dreamy. It was a gorgeous pale pink satin scattered with the sweetest little pink and white daisies, and it had layers and layers of silk petticoats, so it rustled beautifully as I walked. Our tiaras were sparkling on dark blue velvet cushions on our bedside chairs. We were wildly excited . . . until everything went very wrong.

On Thursday morning we had our final test in *Descending the Staircase as if Floating on Air*. All six of us from Rose Room failed miserably, especially me.

Queen Mother Matilda (she's the school's Visiting Expert in

Etiquette,
Posture, Poise,
and Deportment)
got very mad and ordered
us to practice every spare
moment we had.

"If you girls don't improve

dramatically by tomorrow evening," she snapped, "you will spend the day of the Garden Party in your dormitory!" And then she glared at us and swept away.

We did as we were told, but we didn't seem to get any better. By Friday I was *so* worried. What if Queen Mum Mattie said we couldn't go to the Garden Party? That would be terrible, because we'd never get to see the Magical Mirror and win our tiara points!

"My feet hurt!" Charlotte moaned. We dragged ourselves up the Grand Staircase for the hundredth time since breakfast.

"Maybe we'll just *sail* down this time," Katie said hopefully.

"*No* chance," I said gloomily. "I fell over about ten times this morning."

"Head *up*, breathe *in*, *straighten* your back, and *smile*!" Emily and Daisy chanted together.

"And *don't* forget to curtsey on the second-to-bottom step!" Sophia

added as we reached the top landing.

We all groaned loudly.

"Ooooh! Floreen, look!" Nasty Princess Perfecta suddenly appeared with her rotten friend. "It's the dozy rosie-posies!" she said.

Floreen gave us a pitying smile.

"So it is! Isn't it a shame that they're only Perfect Princesses when it comes to *falling* down stairs!" And she and Perfecta sniggered loudly as they went off along the corridor.

I pretended I hadn't heard them and stared out of the window.

Outside in the sunny garden, Princess Moira, Princess Prudence, and Princess Jennifer were running back and forth with armfuls of flowers. Once a week a group of us has to help with the housekeeping (it's supposed to help us run our palaces efficiently when we grow up). They were arranging huge vases of lilies and roses and big white daisies around the courtyard of the Princess Academy.

"Aren't they *lucky*?" I said to Katie. "They passed walking down the stupid staircases last week!"

Katie nodded. "But don't you just hate it when the Grand

Duchess Clara orders you around
every second of the day? And those
horrible aprons. I know they're

supposed to stop our dresses from getting ruined, but they're *so* uncomfortable."

Katie was right about the Grand Duchess being bossy. Prue had obviously put one of the vases in the wrong place in the courtyard, because Duchess Clara was glaring over her spectacles and shaking a silk-gloved finger at her. I could see Prue was trying not to cry as she picked up the vase, and it must have been *really* heavy because she turned bright red as she struggled with it. And then she just happened to look up at the window and saw me looking. She tried *so* hard to smile

at me, and I felt so sorry for her I made a funny face, and pretended to shake my finger like the duchess.

Big mistake!

Prue laughed . . .

. . . and she *dropped* the vase . . .

. . . and it *smashed* into a thousand pieces and *squashed* all the flowers!

And at exactly that moment, I heard a stern voice from the corridor below calling, "Princesses! Let me see you *float* down that staircase!"

Chapter Two

I didn't know what to do! It was completely my fault that Prue had dropped the flowers. I wanted to rush out to the garden, but Queen Mum Mattie was standing at the bottom of the staircase with a grim look on her face.

I made up my mind.

I would float down the staircase, and then dash outside and explain.

"Listen!" I whispered urgently as I pushed in front of Charlotte. "I've got to go first. I've done something awful!"

Then I took a deep breath.

"Head *up*, back *straight*, *smile*!" I said to myself . . . and I tripped on the first step . . . and rolled all the way down . . . and fell right in front of Queen Mother Matilda in a heap.

"Gracious, Princess Alice," she said. "Are you all right?"

"Yes, thank you," I said. "Um— excuse me!" And I ran down the

marble corridor and out through
the garden door.

I found Moira and Jennifer crying
on the steps in a heap of broken
china and crushed flowers.

"Where's the duchess?" I gasped.

Moira sniffed loudly. "She's *furious*! She's stomped off into the kitchen and locked the door."

Jennifer nodded. "She's been in a rotten mood all afternoon because she picked up Queen Mum Mattie's reading glasses at lunch-time instead of her own spectacles. She's sent Prue to polish all the silver, and if we don't clean up this mess and find new flowers by six o'clock we won't be allowed to go to the Garden Party!"

I felt even worse. I was almost certain I wouldn't be going to the Garden Party myself, but this was terrible. I began to pick up some of the flowers, but Jennifer stopped me.

"Don't," she said. "You'll get into trouble if you're seen! You know what the duchess is like. She says we have to learn by our mistakes, or we'll never get to be Perfect Princesses."

And that was when I had a great idea!

"Quick!" I said. "Where's the pantry?"

It was really hard to persuade Prue to let me put on her apron, but I did it in the end. "If I pretend I'm on housekeeping duty I can help Jennifer and Moira while you do the silver," I explained, "and then I'll swap back with you and tell the duchess it was my fault you dropped the vase."

Prue laughed as she picked up

yet another fork. "You did look *just* like Duchess Clara," she said.

"Let's just hope she stays in the kitchen!" I said, as I followed Moira and Jennifer into the garden.

It took us forever to clean up the mess. The pieces of broken china had scattered everywhere, and we had to find every single piece. Then we had to find more flowers, and Jennifer said we weren't supposed to take any without asking the gardeners.

Moira sighed. "I knew it was hopeless. And it's half-past five already."

For a terrible moment I thought Moira was right. And then I had my *second* great idea!

"*I* know!" I said. "Why don't we take just one or two flowers from each of the other vases? I don't think it will show."

So that's what we did. And it didn't take long at all to fill the vase

that Jennifer found in the pantry, and the flowers looked beautiful. You'd never have known there was an accident at all.

"Time for me and Prue to change back again," I said happily.

"I hope she's not too worn out polishing all those knives and forks and spoons!"

But when Moira and Jennifer and I burst into the pantry, there was nothing there but a pile of gleaming silver.

Prudence was *gone*.

Chapter Three

I stood and stared, my eyes popping out of my head. Moira rushed off one way to see if Prue was outside, and Jennifer dashed the other way to see if she was in the kitchen.

Moira came back almost at once, shaking her head.

"She's not there," she said.
And then there was the sharp
tap! tap! tap! of a stick, and Grand

Duchess Clara was standing in front of us. Jennifer was behind her, looking pale.

I tried to look as calm as possible, although my heart was pounding.

"I'm so very sorry," I began, "but it really was all my fault that Princess Prudence broke the vase—"

"What? What's that you're saying?" The duchess leaned forward to peer at me.

I took a deep breath and tried again.

"I was looking out of the window and—"

"Princess Prudence, this is *quite* ridiculous. Princess Moira has just been telling me some foolish story about the garden, and now *you* are talking in riddles." Duchess Clara swept past me and flung open the garden door. Then she stopped

dead as she saw the perfect rows of
flowers.

"*However* did that happen?" she
gasped.

I tried not to look too pleased

with myself. "It was nothing," I said. "And now, if you please, I should find Prue and—"

The duchess turned and stared at me. Then she took off her spectacles and stared again, and an uncomfortable feeling crept into my stomach. She really and truly thought I was Prue!

"Princess Prudence," she said at last, "this is *not* the behavior I would expect from a princess at this academy. I can see the flowers are arranged, and I'm pleased. And you've polished the silver. And I will not prevent you attending the Garden Party tomorrow. But we'll have no more nonsense about you looking for yourself, if you please. I may not have my proper spectacles, but I can still see what's what and who's who. Now, your housekeeping duties are still not finished. Please return to the kitchen!" And she turned and stalked back inside, leaving me staring after her.

"Moira," I said, and I could hear my voice wobbling, "Jennifer— who do *you* think I am?"

"It's okay, Alice," Moira said. "We know who you are. But she's got the wrong glasses on, and she can't see quite right."

Jennifer nodded. "And you do

look a little like Prue. I don't think we should argue with her or she'll get even more furious!"

I couldn't believe my ears. I swallowed hard, but Jennifer and

The Tiara Club

Princess Alice

Go to *www.tiaraclubbooks.com!*
Enter the secret word from each book. Download dazzling
posters you can decorate with your Tiara Club stickers.

KATHERINE TEGEN BOOKS • *An Imprint of* HarperCollins*Publishers* • Sticker art © 2007 by PiART

Moira seized my hands. We had to finish the housekeeping. There was lots of cleaning and dusting and polishing.

Then we had to go into the

kitchen. I'd never even dreamed of a soup pot as big as the one I saw bubbling away on the stove! One of the cooks was stirring it with an enormous wooden spoon.

"Hurry, please!" Duchess Clara ordered. "Everything needs to be out on those trays! Princess Moira—you fetch the bowls! Princess Jennifer—fetch the spoons! Princess Prudence—cut up the bread!"

And there I was, slicing up a loaf of bread as if my life depended on it!

I'd cut up nearly the whole loaf when the duchess came over to see how I was doing.

"Dear me!" she said, and she picked up a slice and peered at it. "This won't do! This won't do at all!"

"It's the best I could do!" I wailed, and I knew I sounded totally pathetic, but I just couldn't help it. My feet hurt, my arms ached, I'd cut my finger, and I was too tired to think of any way of escaping except for just running for it. But then what would happen to the real Prue? She'd be in *such* trouble!

"I'm afraid, Princess Prudence, that your best is not good enough! Please begin again!" And the duchess beckoned to one of the cooks, who slapped another enormous loaf onto the board in front of me.

Did I burst into tears? Almost! But I took a deep breath and told myself I was a Perfect Princess, and I could do it.

I said, "Yes, of course," as politely as I could and gritted my teeth—and started all over again . . .

. . . exactly as there was a *loud* knock on the door. Jennifer ran to open it, and there were my wonderful best friends arm in arm, with Prue hiding behind them. They were all smiling from ear to ear.

Chapter Four

*H*ave you ever tried to hug and be hugged by lots of people at once? It's very difficult, especially when there's a very angry and confused Grand Duchess and a lot of very confused cooks.

"Will somebody *please* tell me

what is going on?" the duchess demanded.

Princess Sophia stepped forward and made one of her deepest curtsies.

"Please forgive us," she said. "We came to thank the cooks for all the truly delicious meals they have given us. We just *love* the stews, and the fishcakes, and the pizza—"

She stopped and looked blank for a second. Charlotte quickly chipped in.

"That's right!" she said, and nudged me hard. I looked around, and Prudence was beckoning to me, her finger on her lips. And while Charlotte, Daisy, Katie, and Emily explained to Grand Duchess Clara how much they appreciated the cooking, Prue and I sneaked into the pantry and I gave her back her apron.

"Thanks for fixing the flowers," Prue whispered. "You're a *star*!"

"Where did you go?" I asked. "I thought I was going to be here forever!"

Prue's eyes twinkled. "After I'd polished the silver I peeked out to

48

see what you were doing," she said, "but you were still busy. So I thought I'd tiptoe back into school and see if I could find the duchess's spectacles for her. And Queen Mum Mattie was making a terrible

fuss because you hadn't come back!"

"Oh dear," I said, and my heart sank. "I'll be in big trouble now."

"No you won't." Prue grinned. "Queen Mother Matilda saw me and thought I was you. She said she hoped I wouldn't fall down the stairs *this* time. And then Daisy whispered to me that you were the only princess who hadn't passed her test!"

I was beginning to feel absolutely sick. "Oh *no*," I moaned. "I'll be the *only* person who can't go to the Garden Party tomorrow."

Prue shook her head and twinkled

even more. "You'll be there, Alice," she said. "I let Queen Mum Mattie continue thinking I was you, and I floated down the staircase. And guess what? She gave me *ten* tiara points!"

"That's right!" Charlotte was standing in the pantry doorway, grinning at us. "Prue was great!"

Prue laughed. "It's a good thing we look a bit alike."

"*And* Katie switched off the main staircase light so Queen Mum Mattie couldn't see properly," Charlotte added.

"Wow!" I could hardly believe it. Prue had passed my test for me, and got me ten tiara points. But a voice was buzzing in my head. *Isn't that cheating?*

And I suddenly felt really uncomfortable, because Prue was looking *so* pleased, and I knew she thought she'd helped me.

"Thank you very much," I said, and I tried to sound as if I meant it.

Prue smiled. "That's okay," she said. "But I'd better run and make sure the duchess doesn't think I've vanished. Oh, and I'll give her her spectacles—that'll cheer her up!"

I limped back to the dining hall with Sophia and the others. My feet were sore, but I didn't mind. It

looked as if I was going to go to the Garden Party after all, *and* I was going to see the Magical Mirror. I just couldn't quite stop that little voice, though. *Perfect Princesses never ever cheat*, it whispered over and over again.

Chapter Five

Perfect Princesses never EVER cheat!

I could hardly sleep that night. I thought and I thought. And when we got up, and dressed in our best dresses, I could hardly breathe. Charlotte said it was excitement, but it was something quite different. I was quaking inside, because I knew what I *had* to do if I was ever going to be a Perfect Princess. I was going to have to own up . . . but not just yet.

My dress was beautiful. It rustled as I slipped it over my head, and when I danced around the skirts swirled and swished. We took turns helping each other with our hair and our tiaras, and then it was time to go across to Fairy G.'s study. We were just in time to see Princess Perfecta and Princess Floreen coming out.

"I'm sure I deserve more tiara points than you," Perfecta was saying angrily.

"I've only got *one* more than you," Floreen said. "I only had—"

Perfecta suddenly noticed us listening. She stopped and glared.

"Shhh!" she snapped at Floreen, and they scuttled away as fast as they could.

We were all feeling really nervous as we knocked on Fairy G.'s door.

Especially me . . .

. . . and then the door opened, and Fairy G. called, "Come in!"

Fairy G. looked wonderful. She doesn't usually dress up, but she was wearing an amazing flowery dress covered in sparkly gold roses. Her long green velvet cloak was embroidered with silver butterflies, and their wings were actually fluttering! You could tell at once that she was a really important Fairy Godmother. We couldn't help curtseying, and she laughed her big, booming laugh.

"Now, Rose Room—do you want to be presented to the mirror one by one, or all together?"

Of course we wanted to be together!

Fairy G. laughed again and

waved her wand, and all of a sudden the shelves full of pots and herbs and potions vanished. Instead we could see an enormous mirror with a strange twisted dark wood frame, and we could see our reflections, standing in a row and holding hands.

"Are you ready?" Fairy G. asked.

I gulped.

"If you please, Fairy G.," I said, and my voice sounded very wobbly. "I have something important to say."

I stepped forward. I could feel my friends staring at me in surprise. "You see," I said, "I've got ten tiara points that aren't really mine. I failed *Descending the Staircase as if Walking on Air*, so I shouldn't be here at all. And I'm very sorry . . ." I had to stop to rub my eyes, ". . . that I didn't say anything before, but I did *so* want to wear my dress, even if it was only for the morning, and now I'll go back to Rose Room and—"

"STOP!"

I couldn't believe it. Fairy G. was actually smiling at me! "I think,

Princess Alice," she said, "we should let the Magical Mirror decide, don't you?" And she waved her wand, and there was an explosion of a million zillion little sparkles of twinkling light. And as we stared in total amazement, a truly beautiful voice spoke to us from the very depths of the mirror.

"Well done, Princess Alice," it said. "You have been honest, and that is an excellent quality in a princess. You must remember that no princess is so perfect that she never makes a mistake." The voice paused and gave a funny little chuckle. "Besides, the Rose Room princesses make me laugh!" For just a second there was a flash of a picture in the mirror—and it was me rolling down the stairs, and my friends staring with big round eyes, and Queen Mum Mattie looking horrified!

Fairy G. gave a little cough.

"Sorry, Fairy G.," the mirror said, "but it *was* funny! Now, where was I? Oh yes. Ahem. I have *much* pleasure in awarding the Princesses Alice, Katie, Daisy, Emily, Charlotte, and Sophia three hundred tiara points to share between them. And, you may *all* go to the Garden Party!"

Chapter Six

What was the Garden Party like? Oh, it was wonderful! And would you believe that I actually did float down the Grand Staircase? I think it must have been because I was so happy! And the flowers in the gardens were glorious. We danced and danced and danced to the music of the orchestra. My grandfather was so pleased the mirror had given me fifty tiara points that he nearly twirled me into a lemonade fountain, but my grandmother caught us just in time.

Late that night, when we were

lying in our beds in Rose Room, I tried yet again to make the others take more tiara points than me, but they wouldn't.

"All for one and one for all," Sophia said sleepily. "And we're *all* going to win enough points to be members of the Tiara Club and have an incredible time."

And I smiled and blew her a kiss . . .

. . . and I'm sending one to you, too.

What happens next?

FIND OUT IN

Princess Sophia
AND THE
Sparkling Surprise

Hello! My name is Princess Sophia, and I'm so pleased you're keeping us company here at the Princess Academy.

Have you met the others from Rose Room? We've been best friends ever since we met on the very first day of school. We take care of each other—a very good thing when there are princesses like Perfecta around.

She's so mean! Some day she'll learn that being a real princess is all about being kind and truthful, and thinking about others before you think of yourself. But until then, Princess Perfecta means trouble!

You are cordially invited to visit www.tiaraclubbooks.com!

Visit your special princess friends at their dazzling website!

Find the secret word hidden in each of the first six Tiara Club books. Then go to the Tiara Club website, enter the secret word, and get an exclusive poster. Print out the poster for each book and save it. When you have all six, put them together to make one amazing poster of the entire Royal Princess Academy. Use the stickers in the books to decorate and make your very own perfect princess academy poster.

More fun at www.tiaraclubbooks.com:

- Download your own Tiara Club membership card!

- Win future Tiara Club books.

- Get activities and coloring sheets with every new book.

- Stay up-to-date with the princesses in this great series!

Visit www.tiaraclubbooks.com and be a part of the Tiara Club!